Out of the City

Leslie Ayvazian

A SAMUEL FRENCH ACTING EDITION

FOUNDED 1830

SAMUELFRENCH.COM
SAMUELFRENCH-LONDON.CO.UK

FOR PRODUCTION ENQUIRIES

UNITED STATES AND CANADA
Info@SamuelFrench.com
1-866-598-8449

UNITED KINGDOM AND EUROPE
Plays@SamuelFrench-London.co.uk
020-7255-4302

Each title is subject to availability from Samuel French, depending upon country of performance. Please be aware that OUT OF THE CITY may not be licensed by Samuel French in your territory. Professional and amateur producers should contact the nearest Samuel French office or licensing partner to verify availability.

MUSIC USE NOTE

OUT OF THE CITY received its first production as part of the Dorset Theatre Festival (Artistic Director, Dina Janis) in Dorset, VT on July 11, 2014. The production was directed by Dina Janis, with set design by Narelle Sissons, costume design by Teresa Snider-Stein, lighting design by Michael Giannitti, and sound design by Will Pickens. The Production Stage Manager was Joanna Obuzor. The cast was as follows:

CAROL	Leslie Ayvazian
MATT	Mark Blum
JILL	John Procaccino
DAN	Janet Zarish

OUT OF THE CITY premiered at Merrimack Repertory Theatre, in Lowell, MA (Charles Towers, Artistic Director; Elizabeth Kegley, Executive Director) in March, 2015. The production was directed by Christian Parker, with scenic design by Lauren Helpern, costume design by Jessica Wegener Shay, lighting design by Brian J. Lilienthal, and sound design by David Remedios. The Production Stage Manager was Casey Leigh Hagwood, and the Assistant Stage Manager was Peter Crewe. The Director of Production was Justin Rowland. The cast was as follows:

CAROL	Charlotte Maier
MATT	Grant Shaud
JILL	Kate Levy
DAN	Ken Land

OUT OF THE CITY originated as a one act play written for Leslie Ayvazian as Carol and Janet Zarish as Jill, performed at the Ensemble Studio Theatre in the Marathon Festival of One Act plays, Spring 2009.

CHARACTERS

Carol and Matt and Jill and Dan are at a Bed & Breakfast for a weekend to celebrate Carol's birthday. These two couples have been friends for many years. Carol is the first to be turning sixty.

SETTING

The lobby of the B&B should indicate the overdone quality of a standard B&B (mismatched upholstery, too many kick-knacks, etc.), but with an eye to suggestion rather than full representation.

The same applies to the only other location, which is a nearby woods next to a lake, which could be defined just by lights.

Some specific things on the set are to be imagined. Example: the fourth wall holds "shelves." The lake scene can be done straight out and doesn't necessarily need its own area. Lights and sounds can define the space. The stones that are thrown into the lake can be invisible, with the sound of the plunk indicating where they land.

The set / the lobby of the Bed & Breakfast, should not be fully enclosed, allowing it to feel porous, as though the outside is present inside.

Ideally, we can see part of a second floor landing and a hallway, and can have a staircase on the set.

AUTHOR'S NOTES

Regarding punctuation: an ellipsis indicates a short breath or beat.

SPECIAL THANKS

Janet Zarish.

Scene One

(It is a morning in late october. The lobby of a B&B. Lights up on **CAROL.** *She's just entered the room. She takes it in. B&B decor isn't her thing. She discovers something notably odd.)*

CAROL. Wow.

(She turns to the fourth wall. She's looking at a "shelf." She gets close to it.)

One, two, three, four, five…six…seven, eight, nine… baskets…a little sailor…Snow White. Dwarf, dwarf, dwarf, dwarf, dwarf, dwarf…uh oh. We're missing a dwarf.

(From offstage we hear her husband, **MATT.***)*

MATT. *(offstage)* CAROL?

CAROL. IN HERE.

MATT. *(offstage)* I'M GOING OUT.

CAROL. DID YOU FIND A MAP?

(He appears.)

MATT. There's a lake. That direction. North.

CAROL. *(still looking at "shelf")* Okay.

MATT. What are you doing?

CAROL. *(pointing)* There are only six dwarves.

MATT. Maybe one ran off to join the things on the lawn.

CAROL. *(little laugh)*

MATT. I'll keep an eye out. *(turns to leave)*

CAROL. We're all going to do something later?

MATT. Dinner?

CAROL. Do you know anything, any plans?

MATT. We have charcoal.

CAROL. Charcoal.

MATT. And vegetables.

CAROL. Tomatoes?

MATT. And corn.

CAROL. Good.

MATT. Okay. *(exits) (offstage)* HAPPY BIRTHDAY.

CAROL. TOMORROW.

MATT. *(offstage)* HAPPY BIRTHDAY TOMORROW!

CAROL. THANKS.

> (**CAROL** *picks up a floor basket – the kind of basket that could hold magazines. She looks around for a place to put the basket. Finds it.*)

You belong here... Better.

> (**DAN** *appears.*)

DAN. Hey!

CAROL. Good morning.

DAN. What's going on?

CAROL. Well, I just moved this from there to here.

DAN. Nice.

CAROL. Thank you.

DAN. Where's Matt?

CAROL. He just left for a walk. He said there's a lake, that direction.

DAN. That direction?

CAROL. Was it that direction?

DAN. I don't know.

CAROL. North!

DAN. Got it.

CAROL. Is Jill upstairs?

DAN. Should be down soon. Having fun?

CAROL. Yeah. Are you?

DAN. Yeah. North?

CAROL. Yeah.

DAN. Catch you later. *(exits)*

CAROL. Bye.

> *(**CAROL** scans the room in hope of finding something to do. She selects a design magazine, sits / starts to read. **JILL** enters in socks, carrying hiking boots.)*

JILL. Good morning.

CAROL. Hi.

JILL. You reading?

CAROL. Just started.

JILL. Happy Birthday!

CAROL. It's tomorrow.

JILL. I know.

CAROL. Are there any plans?

JILL. There will be plans.

CAROL. Dinner?

JILL. Yes.

CAROL. Are those new boots?

JILL. Yes!

CAROL. You going to go hike?

JILL. There's a trail behind the Inn. Come with me.

CAROL. Is it uphill at all?

JILL. It's gentle.

CAROL. Why are you going to wear boots if it's gentle?

JILL. I want to break them in.

CAROL. You're going on another trip.

JILL. I am.

CAROL. You just got back!

JILL. Not really.

CAROL. From the jungle!

JILL. *(looks at soles of boots)* Ooo.

CAROL. What are you looking at?

JILL. The soles of my boots. They have excellent tread.

CAROL. Tread?

JILL. *(putting boot on)* When you walk through a jungle, you have to have tread!

CAROL. Don't tell me why.

JILL. *(lacing boot)* Because everything's wet and covered with insects, so you can't grab on to anything if you start to fall which you might, because you're wearing rubber boots which you thought were a good idea but...the tour people should tell everyone – tread!

CAROL. Tread.

JILL. *(still lacing)* So there we were, walking behind a guide who was swinging a machete through the jungle, making a path so we could get to the Sacred Falls.

CAROL. What made them sacred?

JILL. Wait.

CAROL. Okay.

JILL. And suddenly now, there's a giant boulder blocking our way, and I step on it and I slip because I don't have any tread –

CAROL. *(simultaneously)* Tread

JILL. *(putting other boot on)* Right! So I fall off the boulder and I hit the ground and the guide comes over to me and – Oh! He can't look at me! – eye contact between a native man and an American woman is not allowed – isn't that interesting? – too suggestive they think.

CAROL. That is interesting.

JILL. *(gets up and demonstrates)* So he extends his hand behind him like this. I take it and he pulls me up and then he points to his feet and says, "*Aquí*," and I understand that I am to put my feet on his feet, my forehead on his chest, which I did, and then this man walked me over the boulder and all the way to the Sacred Falls which turned out to be sulfur.

CAROL. Sulfur?

JILL. Yeah.

CAROL. Sacred sulfur?

JILL. Yes. But beautiful.

CAROL. Okay.

JILL. So there we were, in the jungle, at the Falls and it was late. You don't want to be late in a jungle!

CAROL. Oh god.

JILL. The guides told us we didn't have time to walk back to camp. So they led all of us to a nearby river that was narrow and had whirlpools / rapids, and they told us, we had to jump into the river, turn onto our backs and...

CAROL. Don't tell me this part.

JILL. We had to float downstream to our campsite!!

CAROL. Float? You floated in the Amazon River?

JILL. I did!

CAROL. Did your guide friend help you?

JILL. He pulled me by my foot.

CAROL. Did he swim on his back?

JILL. He did.

CAROL. Did he swim with one arm and pull you with the other?

JILL. Yeah. He did!

CAROL. Did you fuck him?

JILL. Carol!

CAROL. Well it sounds all intimate and terrible...

JILL. Did I fuck him? Come on.

CAROL. I'm kidding!

JILL. *(sly)* I thought about it.

CAROL. You're kidding!

JILL. I mean, no. Carol – nothing.

CAROL. *(overlapping)* But...

JILL. *(overlapping)* Nothing, Carol.

CAROL. *(overlapping)* Okay okay.

JILL. *(overlapping)* Come on.

CAROL. What happened to the other group people who didn't have a guide to pull their foot?

JILL. Everyone had someone.

CAROL. Really?

JILL. It always works out.

CAROL. Oh… Where are you going next?

JILL. Macchu Picchu.

CAROL. Macchu Picchu?!

JILL. Christmas break.

CAROL. Does Dan know?

JILL. I'm going to tell him.

CAROL. This weekend?

JILL. Maybe. We'll see. They got up early this morning, our husbands.

CAROL. And went to get charcoal in Sullivan County.

JILL. Sullivan County?

CAROL. I guess they have excellent charcoal.

JILL. In Sullivan County?

CAROL. They stopped at Ffarm Stands on their way back.

JILL. There's a difference in charcoal?

CAROL. I don't know. They got some tomatoes!

JILL. And corn?

CAROL. Yeah.

JILL. Where are they now?

CAROL. Matt went to a lake. And Dan went to join him.

JILL. That's nice.

CAROL. Ya.

JILL. What were you reading?

CAROL. A piece about all the unfinished new buildings.

JILL. They look so stark, don't they, with all the exposed girders. Is that what they are?

CAROL. Girders?

JILL. The metal things. Are they beams?

CAROL. I don't know. Trusses? What's a truss?

JILL. Are they the ones that go this way? *(demonstrates arm at diagonal)*

CAROL. If it's diagonal, it's a truss?

JILL. I don't know. What goes this way? *(arm at right angle)*

CAROL. *(does same gesture)* A column?

JILL. A girder? Which is it?

CAROL. Don't know. *(making arm movements)* Column. Girder. Truss. Is that it?

JILL. I guess so. Why not. *(walks away from CAROL)* This boot is too tight.

CAROL. I think I'm getting tired, a little tired...

JILL. Of?

CAROL. The penis.

JILL. What? Oh. Architecture.

CAROL. You still like it?

JILL. The penis?

CAROL. The penis.

JILL. I do. Don't you?

CAROL. I feel like maybe I've had enough.

JILL. Of the penis?

CAROL. Yeah.

JILL. What does that mean?

CAROL. The insistence of it.

JILL. You don't like that?

CAROL. Not as much.

JILL. You get like this.

CAROL. I do not.

JILL. It's your birthday, you're edgy. I'm worried about this boot.

CAROL. Jill.

JILL. It's a little too tight.

CAROL. I'm turning sixty.

JILL. Maybe if I keep walking around.

CAROL. Sixty!

JILL. You look good.

CAROL. So do you.

JILL. Well, I'm younger and I still like sex.

CAROL. I still like sex.

JILL. But the penis.

CAROL. I'm a little tired.

JILL. Of what? How it looks?

CAROL. Um.

JILL. You forgot how it looks?

CAROL. *(searching for reason)* I don't mind how it looks.

JILL. But you're tired of...?

CAROL. *(it comes to her)* The importance of the erection.

JILL. Really?

CAROL. *(has it!)* I'm tired of my responsibility in keeping things erect.

JILL. Oh come on.

CAROL. I'm tired of pretending I care if things are erect.

JILL. Things have to be erect.

CAROL. Why?

> (**JILL** *picks up a strange looking glittery trinket.*)

JILL. Ooooo

CAROL. What is that?

JILL. It's a gourd with rhinestones.

CAROL. It is, isn't it.

JILL. Yes.

CAROL. It needs to be featured.

> *(takes it from her)*

JILL. Of course.

CAROL. *(looking for place to put gourd)* Why do things have to be erect?

JILL. If things aren't erect, things will collapse.

CAROL. *(still looking for place)* So what if things collapse?

JILL. Then things will be horizontal.

CAROL. It could be nice if things were horizontal. *(placing gourd)* That's good.

JILL. *(looking at her feet)* What socks did I wear in the store?

CAROL. We wouldn't have to look up. We could look out or down, like the men in that jungle of yours.

JILL. Looking up can inspire.

CAROL. Inspire what?

JILL. Hope. You know – hope.

> *(**JILL** gestures with arms up – hope.)*

CAROL. Or it can strain your neck. Where are you going?

JILL. *(exiting)* Over here, this room. It's called the Breakfast Room.

CAROL. How do you know everything?

JILL. *(offstage)* I READ THE PAMPHLETS.

CAROL. WHAT PAMPHLETS?

JILL. *(offstage)* IN THE BASKET.

CAROL. WHICH BASKET?

JILL. *(offstage)* YOU WANT SOME TEA?

CAROL. NOT RIGHT NOW.

JILL. *(offstage)* THEY HAVE LITTLE BOXES OF CORNFLAKES.

CAROL. *(finds pamphlets)* Pamphlets.

JILL. *(offstage)* ARE YOU EATING CARBS?

CAROL. UH…

JILL. *(offstage)* NO?

CAROL. NO THANKS.

JILL. *(enters with tea)* I think the boot guy gave me the wrong boots.

CAROL. Maybe the boot guy's clairvoyant. Maybe he's saying – "Enough trips for you, Girl from Queens." *(crossing to)* Breakfast Room!

JILL. I can't tell if I should take these back.

CAROL. *(offstage in Breakfast Room)* There's fruit, and nuts, and…

JILL. Have you ever had sex with a woman?

CAROL. *(enters)* Oh… No. Have you?

JILL. No.

CAROL. I almost did. In Ohio. She lived upstairs.

JILL. Why didn't you?

CAROL. The moment passed. Does it seem like a big deal to you?

JILL. Not really. But I know what you mean.

CAROL. What do you know that I mean?

JILL. I don't know.

CAROL. Would you be with a woman if…

JILL. I've thought of us living together.

CAROL. I've thought about that.

JILL. I could see us ending up together on a couch under a blanket in our later years.

CAROL. Oh. You mean… If…well… I won't finish that sentence.

JILL. Yeah, right, no.

CAROL. I know, but, I mean, how would it be, do you think, if we lived together?

JILL. You mean what, the house?

CAROL. Not so much the house.

JILL. You mean, us?

CAROL. Yeah.

JILL. Role wise?

CAROL. Would there be roles?

JILL. People who live together seem to have roles.

CAROL. In that case, I'm probably the more butch one.

JILL. Why are you the more butch?

CAROL. Because I'm brunette.

JILL. Come on!

CAROL. I know, but I think I am the more butch.

JILL. I'm a bit butch.

CAROL. No.

JILL. What is butch?

CAROL. Tailored?

JILL. Tailored?

CAROL. I don't know. We don't know. What do we know?

JILL. We know you're tired of pricks.

CAROL. Maybe. Maybe I just wanted to say penis in this room.

JILL. Why?

CAROL. Because this room is flowery.

JILL. I like it.

CAROL. That's 'cause you're fem. Where is everyone?

JILL. It's the off-season.

CAROL. *(unsettled)* Are we the only ones here?

JILL. I don't know.

CAROL. ...Jill?

JILL. Let's go outside.

CAROL. Remember my fiftieth birthday party?

JILL. Come on, Carol.

CAROL. I made that speech. I said I was content.

JILL. I remember.

CAROL. Why did I say that?

JILL. You thought it was true.

CAROL. Why did I think that?

JILL. Hope?

CAROL. Hope? *(mimics* JILL*'s earlier gesture but without looking up)*

JILL. Gimme your hand. I'll pull you up. We can walk.

> *(*JILL *takes* CAROL*'s hand,* CAROL *does not stand.)*

CAROL. Hi.

JILL. Hi.

CAROL. Do you think I'm sexy? I don't believe I just asked you if you think...

JILL. *(overlapping)* Yes, you're sexy, Carol. Do you think I'm sexy…

CAROL. Of course. I get a kick walking with you. I watch other people and I think – yeah, she's my friend and I know what you see.

JILL. Ohh really? Thank you. Aw.

CAROL. Jill…

JILL. What.

CAROL. I'm thinking of the time I called you from Mexico City.

JILL. Oh God.

CAROL. You hadn't worried.

JILL. Denial. Carol.

CAROL. It was headline news. For several days.

JILL. I thought you had left for L.A.

CAROL. We hadn't.

JILL. No.

CAROL. What about all the times I've thought of you in the jungle or the river? And Matt and I go to Mexico City – we're there one day, they have an earthquake and you don't notice.

JILL. I listened to the news. I knew about the earthquake. I knew you were in Mexico. I didn't make the connection.

CAROL. Why not?!

JILL. In my mind, you were safe. When you called to say, "I'm safe." I didn't know what you were talking about. You kept saying, "I'm safe," and I didn't get it!

CAROL. A person wants to think…

JILL. Carol. How many years?

CAROL. That doesn't matter.

JILL. It was 1985.

CAROL. Okay. Okay. One more thing. You don't contact me when you're away.

JILL. Oh God.

CAROL. You say: "I'll call."

JILL. I don't want to talk. Even on days when I'm worn out or lonely, I don't want to call anyone.

CAROL. But Dan.

JILL. I talk to Dan.

CAROL. Then don't tell me you'll call.

JILL. I… Fair.

CAROL. Fair.

JILL. All right.

CAROL. What are you doing?

JILL. I want to go for a walk!

CAROL. Jill…

JILL. What?

CAROL. Do you think men are delicate?

JILL. Sure. Do you?

CAROL. Yes.

JILL. Carol. So what?

CAROL. Do you think Dan needs to hear that you love him?

JILL. I tell him I love him.

CAROL. Is it different since the kids left the house?

JILL. What are you getting at?

CAROL. I don't know.

JILL. You seem…

CAROL. Agitated.

JILL. Yes.

CAROL. I'm turning sixty!

JILL. People turn sixty.

CAROL. People do things when they turn sixty. Some people travel. You.

JILL. I've always traveled.

CAROL. Some people enjoy the fruits of their labor. Some people aren't so sure of their fruits. I mean, there's family, of course, but I have this sense, that I'm… waiting, still, I mean, I…uh, ick, ehh… *(Disgusted with her self pity, she can't find the words)*

JILL. Carol, Listen…

CAROL. I'm going to ask you not to be annoyed.

JILL. I was going to point things out.

CAROL. Please don't point things out.

JILL. Good things.

CAROL. Please don't. *(sighs / looks up)* Oh!

JILL. What?

CAROL. *(looks down quickly)* Do you ever get dizzy?

JILL. What?

CAROL. When you look up?

JILL. Did you see a doctor?

> (**JILL** *sits next to or across from* **CAROL.**)

CAROL. I have dislodged crystals in my inner ear.

JILL. What?

CAROL. I don't want dislodged crystals.

JILL. You want your crystals lodged.

CAROL. I do.

JILL. Of course.

CAROL. The nurse suggested I name things in the room to ground me.

JILL. Like…frilly lamp shades.

CAROL. Baskets.

JILL. Pillows.

CAROL. Conch.

JILL. What?

CAROL. *(points)* A conch. Over there. *(inhales / dizziness gone)*

JILL. Oh. The shell.

> (*Both laugh.*)

CAROL. Yeah.

JILL. It's nice.

CAROL. Yeah.

JILL. *(turns to* **CAROL***)* Happy Birthday.

(They are close, face to face.)

CAROL. Did you buy me a present?

JILL. I bought you a present.

CAROL. What is it?

(Faces are close.)

JILL. An afgan. It's very soft.

CAROL. Do I need that?

JILL. I don't know.

(Beat. Slowly a kiss happens. It shouldn't be clear who initiates it. It's a soft kiss. Just their mouths are touching. It lasts a bit. Kiss ends. Beat.)

CAROL. I have an afghan.

JILL. This one is nicer.

CAROL. Okay.

JILL. ...So. Tonight, fresh corn.

CAROL. And tomatoes.

JILL. Purchased by our husbands.

CAROL. Along with very good charcoal.

JILL. Superior charcoal.

CAROL. Maybe they found superior charcoal.

JILL. *(stands)* Yeah. Okay! I'm going out. What are you going to do?

CAROL. Maybe I'll read. I don't know.

JILL. Okay.

CAROL. Should we...

JILL. What?

CAROL. Talk?

JILL. Do you want to talk?

CAROL. What do you think?

JILL. I think... I want to walk.

CAROL. Fresh air?

JILL. Yeah.

CAROL. Okay.

JILL. Then we'll talk.

CAROL. Okay.

JILL. See you. Soon.

CAROL. Yeah.

> (*JILL exits. Beat. **CAROL**, a little unnerved looks around the room for something to re-arrange. She sees the conch. Decides to move it next to the couch. She stands back to evaluate.*)

Conch. Couch. (*knows this is ridiculous*) Oh for Pete's sake!

> (*She picks up magazine and walks out.*)

Scene Two

(We hear the sound of a rock being thrown into a lake. Plunk. Lights up on a "wooded area." **MATT** *is looking at a lake. He has been throwing rocks at a log in the lake. He aims / he throws. We hear another plunk. Frustrated, he picks up another rock and prepares to throw.* **CAROL** *enters.)*

CAROL. Matt.

MATT. *(surprised)* What!

CAROL. Hi.

MATT. I didn't hear you.

CAROL. You trying to hit that log?

MATT. Yeah.

CAROL. Where's Dan?

MATT. I don't know. He left.

CAROL. Did you both throw rocks at the log?

MATT. Yes.

CAROL. Did he hit it?

MATT. He hit it.

CAROL. Well, he's athletic. I mean he's a coach! How's your arm?

MATT. *(looking for more rocks)* It's okay.

CAROL. Can you stop doing that?

MATT. In a minute.

CAROL. Can you look at me?

MATT. Wait. *(finds rock)*

CAROL. Matt?

MATT. Okay. *(stops, looks at her)* What's up?

CAROL. How do I look?

MATT. Nice. *(turns back to set up throw)*

CAROL. Matt!

MATT. I just have to hit that log.

CAROL. Matt…

MATT. Just one time.

CAROL. Your arm doesn't hurt?

MATT. It's okay. *(throws rock, misses, plunk)* Damn!

CAROL. Matt, please pay more attention to me.

MATT. Okay. What?

CAROL. Do you like it here?

MATT. This spot?

CAROL. The Bed and Breakfast.

MATT. *(looking for another rock)* I liked the breakfast.

CAROL. What was it?

MATT. French toast.

CAROL. I had the omelet.

MATT. I know. *(throws rock, misses, plunk)* EH!

CAROL. Was it real maple syrup?

MATT. *(finds another rock)* I think so.

CAROL. Are you going to keep throwing rocks?

MATT. Yes. *(throws rock, misses, plunk)* Damn.

CAROL. Are we going to spend time on my birthday weekend looking for a cold compress and a hot water…

MATT. Aspirin.

CAROL. I have aspirin.

MATT. *(back to looking for rocks)* Then we'll be fine.

CAROL. Except you'll be quiet.

MATT. I'll talk.

CAROL. But you'll be thinking about the log.

MATT. No I won't.

CAROL. You know you were told not to lift your arm / where are you going?

MATT. *(moves offstage)* Over here.

CAROL. More rocks?

MATT. Yeah.

CAROL. Matt!

MATT. *(comes back on)* What do you want to do?

CAROL. There's a trail behind the Inn.

MATT. You want to hike?

CAROL. Well. Walk.

MATT. Did you bring sneakers?

CAROL. I have these. They're fine.

MATT. You want to walk? Where did you say? Behind the Inn? *(throws rock, misses, plunk)*

CAROL. Matt, what if I grab you and force you to stop.

MATT. *(looks for rocks)* I'll break free.

CAROL. What if I'm suddenly very strong?

MATT. I'll be suddenly very stronger.

CAROL. *(playful)* What if I hit your arm!

MATT. You can't hit my arm.

CAROL. What if I do, what if... *(hits arm)* there...

MATT. HEY. You hit my arm.

CAROL. Out of love!

MATT. That was twisted.

CAROL. Does it hurt?

MATT. That was twisted.

CAROL. Give us a kiss!

MATT. For Pete's sake.

> *(He kisses her, then holds her and slowly positions her so that he can see the lake over her shoulder. She knows he's looking at the log.)*

CAROL. What if I threw the rock at the log?

MATT. What?

CAROL. *(breaks from hug)* What if we decided my arm was your arm!

MATT. We won't decide that.

CAROL. *(enthusiastic)* Wouldn't it be great, if in a marriage...

MATT. *(overlapping)* Don't say this, Carol, whatever this is...

CAROL. *(eager to convince him)* Wait wait... If in a marriage, when one member is experiencing for example, a weak arm and...

MATT. *(overlapping)* Don't say weak arm, Carol, come on...

CAROL. *(overlapping)* Wait wait wait Matt, if one member of the couple has, for example, an arm that is healing from an accident that meant he could NOT...

MATT. Don't say accident...

CAROL. Raise his arm.

MATT. Don't say arm.

CAROL. He could not comb his hair!

MATT. Don't talk about this.

CAROL. *(overlapping)* Wait! Wait! What if the other member could throw the rock for the healing member and the healing member could feel...

MATT. Don't talk about members!

CAROL. The healing person could feel satisfied!!!

MATT. Don't say these words, Carol, okay? Just let your husband throw his rock. *(throws, misses, plunk)*

CAROL. Oh no!

MATT. What?

CAROL. I heard the click!

MATT. You didn't.

CAROL. I did. You know I did.

MATT. The click.

CAROL. You fell in the hall! You cracked the bone! Your arm has a click!

MATT. It's better.

CAROL. You wore socks to bed.

MATT. *(picks up another rock)* I can tell it's better.

CAROL. Briefs. T-shirts. Socks!

MATT. You don't have to worry.

CAROL. Socks!

MATT. I'm doing fine. *(throws, misses, plunk)*

CAROL. That's why you fell!

MATT. *(stares at log)* Damn.

CAROL. I can't tell how far that log is, but I think it's too far. Matt, the log is too far.

MATT. No it's not! Sometimes I throw and it's overshot.

CAROL. Matt!

MATT. What? Happy Birthday.

CAROL. What?

MATT. This is your weekend.

CAROL. *(mattter of fact)* It's hard to know, isn't it, after all these years, what to do with a birthday.

MATT. It's hard to know what to do with your birthday.

CAROL. You aren't sixty.

MATT. Other people are sixty and they're fine. The sun's coming out.

CAROL. *(looks up/ feels dizzy)* Sun? Oh! Okay. *(looks down)* Rock. Dirt. Forest growth.

MATT. What are you doing?

CAROL. Naming things.

MATT. Why?

CAROL. It helps me ground. *(inhales / dizziness gone)*

MATT. Oh… Okay. *(picks up rock)*

CAROL. Matt!

MATT. It's not the distance.

CAROL. Did I say distance?

MATT. Yes you did!

CAROL. *(conceding)* Yes I did.

MATT. Carol, just let me do this! Please go away so I can throw this one rock!

CAROL. …Fine.

> *(She leaves.* **MATT** *prepares to throw. She returns.)*

Explain it to me! Matt, please explain it to me! Matt! Come on!

MATT. You come on! Just let me hit the log!!!

CAROL. No!

MATT. Yes!

CAROL. It's insane!!

MATT. So what?!

CAROL. I don't want you to be insane!! Matt! Talk!

MATT. You want me to talk now?!

CAROL. Yes!!

MATT. Okay! ...Okay. It's about the moment you hear the sound of contact and the sound after contact, which is silence. No. That isn't it. Here it is – At a certain point, this rock becomes a referendum.

CAROL. What does that mean?

MATT. This rock is the Universe saying: "You will triumph, Matthew." It's – "You hit the elk, the elk goes down and the tribe eats."

CAROL. The tribe eats?

MATT. It's the bell rings, you win the prize, you kiss the girl and she says: "You are my hero." And once you commit to it, every time the rock sinks into oblivion, the universe says, "Sorry Guy, maybe the next elk, the next tribe, the next life." I can't accept the death of my tribe because of my inability to throw a rock.

CAROL. Wow.

MATT. Yeah.

CAROL. Huh.

MATT. Yeah.

CAROL. Matt...

MATT. What?

CAROL. Can't you hit the elk and save the tribe while I stand here and watch?

MATT. No.

CAROL. No?

MATT. I can't.

CAROL. What if I were a young tribal girl?

MATT. What?

CAROL. What if we were a young tribal couple?

MATT. Okay.

CAROL. And you brought me to this glade. And there was an elk by the log.

MATT. In the water?

CAROL. Maybe there wasn't water, but there were rocks, these exact rocks. And I said to you, "Matthew I love you, will you kill that elk?"

MATT. And I would say, "I will kill that elk."

CAROL. "Okay, good!" I would say.

MATT. And I would say, "I'm glad you're happy."

CAROL. So the question is: Could you kill the elk with me standing here – the young me, the dewy me?

MATT. The dewy you?

CAROL. Yes.

MATT. Maybe the young dewy me could snatch up a rock like a baseball and throw it ninety-five miles an hour at the elk's head and boom it goes down.

CAROL. And would I say, "You are my hero?!"

MATT. Yes.

CAROL. And if it happened that it were my birthday, would you give me the elk?

MATT. Would I give you...

CAROL. Matt!

MATT. Okay yeah, sure.

CAROL. So you'd get another elk for the tribe?

MATT. I'd have to.

CAROL. Two elks?

MATT. I'd try.

CAROL. Thank you.

MATT. Sure thing.

CAROL. But now – Carol, the Crone of the tribe, has to stumble off by herself and find something to do while you, the aging hunter comes to grips with the rock that is the universe.

MATT. *(half-hearted)* Why don't you stay.

CAROL. No. Thanks. *(turns to exit / turns back: definitive)* Come find me.

MATT. Okay.

(She leaves.)

MATT. Carol?

*(**MATT** considers following her. Then looks at the log, aims, throws the rock. We hear it hit the log. He raises his arms in triumph.)*

I hit it!

Scene Three

*(The lobby of the Bed and Breakfast. **DAN** enters.)*

DAN. JILL?

*(**DAN** enters / looks at his watch.)*

9:35. In the Poconos. Now what? Uh. *(looks around)* The Breakfast Room. Let's try that.

*(**DAN** exits. **CAROL** enters with magazine. She's looking for **JILL**. She puts magazine on coffee table. **JILL** enters. They look at each other. It's charged.)*

JILL. Hi!

CAROL. Hi!

JILL. Hi. I mean what are you doing?

CAROL. I'm returning the magazine. What are you doing?

JILL. Have you seen Dan? Is he around?

CAROL. I haven't seen him.

JILL. Where did they go?

CAROL. To the lake. They're at the lake.

JILL. Still?

CAROL. I don't know, I have no idea…

JILL. Carol!

CAROL. What? I know! What?

*(**JILL** crosses to **CAROL**. She grabs **CAROL** by her wrists. They speak in heightened whispered voices.)*

JILL. Carol!

CAROL. What?

JILL. We're friends thirty years…

CAROL. I know.

JILL. Our kids are friends. Our husbands. Carol, over thirty years.

CAROL. I know.

JILL. I was hiking, it's a little grey out and I was up behind the Inn, have you been out…

CAROL. Yes.

JILL. I was looking for stones – I wanted to build a marker to find my way back – did you notice the sun tried to come out for a bit – and I found a stone, a very smooth one and I thought, this stone's for Carol and then I kissed it. Carol.

CAROL. You kissed the stone?

JILL. And I thought, if I gave it to you, would you put it to your lips. Too?

CAROL. Would I kiss the stone?

JILL. Sounds crazy!

CAROL. Do you have it?

JILL. No.

CAROL. You left it there?

JILL. I could find it again. Do you want it?

CAROL. I, um, I could paint it.

JILL. Paint it?

CAROL. Oh, Jill – I don't know!

JILL. Carol. Carol!

CAROL. I know!

JILL. Have we become lesbians this weekend?

CAROL. Jill…

JILL. Do I look like a lesbian?

CAROL. You look the same.

JILL. Do I look flushed?

CAROL. You look rosy.

JILL. Not flushed?

CAROL. Well, maybe.

JILL. Put your forehead on mine.

CAROL. Jill, no, let's not…let's…

JILL. Let's put our foreheads, our foreheads, come on…

     (**JILL** *bows her head.*)

CAROL. Why are we putting our foreheads…

JILL. Because we need to…

CAROL. But we don't know where everyone...

JILL. No one's around. Everyone left.

CAROL. Everyone left?

JILL. I think so.

CAROL. Where did they go?

JILL. I don't know. Errands, bowling?

CAROL. Bowling?

JILL. I don't know, maybe the people who run this place bowl.

CAROL. *(not whispering)* Jill, we can't lose our minds!

JILL. Shhh!

CAROL. Why are we whispering!

JILL. Just cause we're whispering.

CAROL. Oh Jill.

> (CAROL *puts her forehead on* JILL'*s.* JILL *is still holding* CAROL'*s wrists. They stand forehead to forehead.)*

JILL. Am I warm?

CAROL. A little.

JILL. You're warm too.

CAROL. Maybe we had a surge. *(lifts her head, looks at* JILL*)*

JILL. *(looking at* CAROL*)* You mean a flash?

CAROL. I don't know...

JILL. *(bowing head)* Put your head back.

CAROL. Oh God.

> *(puts her forehead on* JILL'*s forehead)*

JILL. Carol...

CAROL. *(whispering)* Shh. Be quiet. I think we should be quiet.

JILL. *(whispering)* Do you think...

> (DAN *enters. He stands in doorway. He overhears:)*

CAROL. *(whispering)* Sh. Let's not attract attention.

JILL. *(whispering)* But...

DAN. Good morning?

>*(They break apart.)*

JILL. Dan!

CAROL. Hi!

JILL. Hi Dan.

DAN. Hi.

JILL. Where were you?

DAN. I was outside. And then I was in the Breakfast Room. *(points to it)* That room.

JILL. Uh-huh.

DAN. I had some walnuts.

JILL. Walnuts.

DAN. I was going to have a banana but I don't like bananas. Am I interrupting?

JILL. No no. We were just talking.

CAROL. Have you seen Matt?

DAN. He was at the lake. What's going on?

JILL. Where's the lake?

CAROL. That direction. *(points wrong direction)*

DAN. *(points correct direction)* That direction.

JILL & CAROL. Oh. Yeah.

CAROL. *(to DAN)* You were there too, right, Dan?

DAN. For a few minutes.

CAROL. *(to JILL)* They were throwing rocks at a log.

JILL. Fun! Right? So, what are you doing?

DAN. I'm looking for you.

JILL. Oh good.

CAROL. Why don't I go find Matt and we'll all meet up here? Later?

JILL. And later, we'll...

CAROL. Yeah...we'll...

JILL. Dinner.

CAROL. Yeah.

JILL. Salmon?

CAROL. Good. See you.

    (She exits.)

DAN. …New boots?

JILL. *(grateful for change of subject)* Yeeesss! *(stomps the floor)* Boots!

DAN. Breaking them in?

JILL. I've been, yes, *(stomps floor)* trying to break them in.

DAN. When were you going to tell me?

JILL. Tell you what?

DAN. I know what new boots mean.

JILL. Oh. I'm thinking of going to Macchu Picchu.

DAN. Peru.

JILL. Yes.

DAN. When?

JILL. Christmas break. Do you want to come?

DAN. Do I want to go to Macchu Picchu?

JILL. Yeah.

DAN. Hello, I'm Dan. I'm a coach at the High School.

JILL. *(overlapping)* Ha ha.

DAN. I'm your husband. We have two children, we're fond of them.

JILL. Dan!

DAN. When was the last time you asked me to go on a trip?

JILL. I don't remember. Why are you wearing your jacket?

DAN. I thought I'd go find a court.

JILL. Shoot some hoops?

DAN. Yes.

JILL. What's in your hand?

DAN. Car keys.

JILL. Put them down.

DAN. Put them down?

JILL. Free up your hands.

DAN. Why?

JILL. Come on.

DAN. All right. There.

JILL. Let's kiss.

DAN. You want a kiss?

JILL. Yeah.

DAN. Now?

JILL. Come on. *(stomps her foot on floor)*

DAN. You breaking those boots in?

JILL. I'm trying. *(stomps again)* How do I look?

DAN. I admit there's something compelling.

JILL. *(stomps)* The boots?

DAN. Don't know if it's the boots or the legs in the boots.

JILL. *(stomps)* Are we verging on something?

DAN. I don't know. Where is everyone?

JILL. It's the off-season.

DAN. Are we the only ones…

JILL. I don't know. Come here!

DAN. You're summoning?

JILL. Let's kiss.

DAN. Now?

JILL. You come to me.

DAN. Okay. OKAY. *(starts to cross)*

JILL. Wait!

DAN. What?!

JILL. I'll turn away.

DAN. Turn away?

JILL. Then you can grab my arm and pull me back.

DAN. Pull you back where?

JILL. Pull me to you. Pull me hard.

DAN. Pull you hard?!

JILL. Try it. Please try it.

DAN. Okay.

JILL. Okay. Go.

> (She turns away, he reaches and steps but he misses her arm.)

Dan?

DAN. Yeah. I muffed it.

JILL. Try again, Okay?

DAN. Okay. Go!

JILL. Okay. *(turns away)*

> (He grabs her with force and pulls her to him. They are close, face to face.)

DAN. Hey!

JILL. Hey.

DAN. Hello... Say hello.

JILL. Hello.

DAN. Say: You are my sweetheart.

JILL. You are my sweetheart.

> (He kisses her. It is another simple kiss – not full bodied. Kiss ends. JILL looks at him.)

Dan...

DAN. What?!

JILL. Do you think...?

DAN. Think what?

JILL. Could you, when we kiss, could you...

DAN. Could I what?

JILL. Soften your mouth.

DAN. Oh my God.

JILL. I mean, could you, just, the bottom lip...

DAN. What about it?

JILL. Could you give it to me?

DAN. What does that mean?

JILL. Could you, you know *(starts demonstrating / pushing her lip out)* could you make it...or let it be...fleshy.

DAN. You don't like my lip?

JILL. I love your lip, just could you…

DAN. Twenty-eight years and you want…

JILL. *(overlapping)* Can we just try…

DAN. *(overlapping)* Fleshy?

JILL. Fleshy / Fat. Remember when our lips were fat?

DAN. Fat?!

JILL. Like a peach.

DAN. Oh my God!!

JILL. Dan?

DAN. What?

JILL. Come on.

DAN. What?!

JILL. Kiss me. Just kiss me!

DAN. You gotta be kidding.

JILL. Please.

DAN. I already kissed you.

JILL. Again.

DAN. No I can't.

JILL. Dan.

DAN. I'm going to drive into town. Find a court.

JILL. Now?

DAN. I can still shoot a one-hander from the mid-court line. Did you know that?

JILL. I…well… I… Yes.

DAN. *(doesn't believe her)* Right… *(turns to exit)*

JILL. Dan!

DAN. *(turns back)* You weren't talking.

JILL. What?

DAN. You and Carol. When I walked in.

JILL. Oh.

DAN. You were whispering.

JILL. I was comforting her.

DAN. Standing like that?

JILL. You know it's her birthday and she's agitated because…

DAN. I know the birthday situation…

JILL. Okay!

DAN. Comforting her?

JILL. Yes.

DAN. That's the whole story?

JILL. Yeah.

DAN. Okay. *(starts to exit)* I'm going.

JILL. To find a court?

DAN. *(exiting)* Yeah.

JILL. Where?

DAN. *(offstage)* WE'LL SEE WHAT'S OUT THERE.

JILL. DAN, THIS DOESN'T NEED TO BE UNSETTLING.

> *(***DAN*** *re-appears.)*

DAN. Say that again?

JILL. This doesn't need to be unsettling.

DAN. Good to know.

> *(***DAN*** *exits.* ***JILL*** *stays.)*

JILL. …Um.

> *(***MATT*** *enters. He's still thinking of his triumph with the rock and log. His elbow tingles. It is inflamed again.)*

JILL. *(startled)* Hi.

MATT. Hi. What are you doing?

JILL. Fine. I mean, nothing – standing here! How are you?

MATT. I'm fine too. Do you know where Carol is?

JILL. I think she's looking for you.

MATT. Do you know where she went?

JILL. I don't know.

MATT. Okay, well, I'm going to sit down. She'll come back here, right?

(He is trying to put his arm in a comfortable position.)

JILL. Sure yeah. There's a magazine – there, it has an interesting story about new construction, if you want... Are you all right?

MATT. Yes. Thanks. Maybe I'll take a look at the magazine.

JILL. Okay.

MATT. Are there plans for a party?

JILL. I'm playing with menus.

MATT. She likes salmon.

JILL. Is that special, you think?

MATT. Well, we'll grill it.

JILL. Of course.

MATT. Okay.

JILL. Good. See you later.

MATT. Right.

JILL. Bye.

MATT. Bye.

(JILL exits. MATT sits on couch, picks up magazine, doesn't open it. He's recalling the rock and log.)

Scene Four

(DAN enters. He's looking for his car keys. Sees them.)

DAN. Keys! *(gets them)* Hey Matt.

MATT. *(startled)* Hi.

DAN. You were staring.

MATT. Oh. Yeah.

DAN. You okay?

MATT. I hit the log. Finally!

DAN. Finally counts. I'll see you later.

MATT. Where you going?

DAN. Gonna look for a court.

MATT. Did you get Carol a present?

DAN. Me?

MATT. I mean will there be presents?

DAN. You got her one, right?

MATT. Well...

DAN. Uh oh.

MATT. She told me she'd lost her favorite black jacket. So I asked her how it was different from her other black jackets. She said it was not really black, it was navy blue and hadn't I noticed since I'm a graphic designer.

DAN. Got it.

MATT. I thought I would find her another navy blue jacket that looks almost black,

DAN. But you didn't.

MATT. I don't know her size. And I...

DAN. Couldn't ask her.

MATT. I mean she'd be fine. But...

DAN. You couldn't ask her.

MATT. No.

DAN. What'd you get?

MATT. Soaps.

DAN. Don't tell me soaps.

MATT. Lots of soaps. Every scent. And a loofah.

DAN. The loofah is good.

MATT. What do you get for Jill?

DAN. Clothes that flick moisture.

MATT. Clothes…?

DAN. That flick moisture.

MATT. What are those?

DAN. Tee-shirts, panties, socks. For her hikes.

MATT. Was that her idea?

DAN. I think it was mine. You know I went with her once.

MATT. Right. Where was it?

DAN. Mongolia! Rocky terrain. Very rocky terrain. She'd go for a walk and select two or three rocks from one hundred million and bring them back to the place where we stayed which was a Yurt.

MATT. Right.

DAN. Which is a circular tent.

MATT. I remember the pictures. It's Spartan.

DAN. She would display the rocks on the floor of the yurt which was Compressed Dirt.

MATT. I recall. Dan – let me ask you…

DAN. About the yurt?

MATT. No. Unless you want to talk more…

DAN. No I'm done.

MATT. Okay, here, let me ask you – Do you think there's an expectation when on vacation like Mongolia, or even on a weekend like this one, for something special?

DAN. Like…

MATT. Like the soaps. Are they romantic?

DAN. Romantic? Uh. Lather is sexy. Do you two take baths?

MATT. We shower.

DAN. Lather is tricky in showers.

MATT. Yes it is. Let me ask this…okay…it's okay?

DAN. I'm not sure where the hell we're headed, but...

MATT. Okay. So, what am I asking?

DAN. Soap?

MATT. No.

DAN. Lather?

MATT. Sex.

DAN. Sex?

MATT. The act.

DAN. We're talking about the act of sex?

MATT. Is that okay?

DAN. What part of sex?

MATT. The organ?

DAN. The penis?

MATT. The woman.

DAN. The woman's organ?

MATT. Yeah.

DAN. Which one?

MATT. The clitoris? *(pronounced cliTORis)*

DAN. Okay... Isn't it CLIToris?

MATT. Is that what you say?

DAN. I say clit, when I discuss it, which is never.

MATT. I know.

DAN. Except wait – I had a buddy, college, Irish guy, he called it *(accent)*: "The little man in the boat."

MATT. *(accent)* Little man in a boat.

DAN. *(accent)* The little man in the boat.

MATT. That's good.

DAN. Right!

MATT. So tell me this – does it stand up and salute like it once did?

DAN. Stand up and...

MATT. Oh My God!

DAN. What?!

MATT. We think female genitalia is a little dude!

DAN. No we don't.

MATT. That's what we just said…

DAN. We didn't mean it.

MATT. How do we know we didn't mean it?

DAN. Why would we mean it? And who talks like this?

MATT. Carol does. It's infectious.

DAN. No it isn't. I gotta go.

MATT. Wait. Just let me ask this… Have you noticed, with your wife, with Jill –

DAN. Jill, right.

MATT. Have you noticed, does Jill care, for example, when you show any sign of…distraction, let's call it distraction.

DAN. Distraction. Like what?

MATT. I mean for example…

DAN. Yeah?

MATT. Here's an example: I put my hand to my chin and Carol thinks I've tuned out.

DAN. Have you?

MATT. I can still hear.

DAN. Okay, so, I guess the question is, can you remember to leave your hands in your lap?

MATT. That's the question?

DAN. I don't know, buddy. Habits are habits.

MATT. Does Jill…?

DAN. Jill tends not to be critical. Except lately. Today. Maybe not critical. Maybe instructive.

MATT. Instructive?

DAN. Maybe, a little instructive.

MATT. Uh-huh… Dan…

DAN. Is this another question?

MATT. Did you know, as women age, they gain testosterone!

DAN. Did not know that.

MATT. Men lose. Women gain. How about that?

DAN. Can we discuss this another time, like in twenty years, because...

MATT. But, wait, do you think there might be some greater plan to reversing positions? That's the question! Women gain testosterone and men lose testosterone! – Is there something correct about that?

DAN. Off the bat – no. There's nothing correct about that. I don't see the evidence and I don't want to see the evidence...

MATT. *(overlapping)* Have you ever noticed...

DAN. Oh God.

MATT. How older men's faces get softer?

DAN. Softer? No.

MATT. Some men resemble Eleanor Roosevelt!

DAN. No! Nooo.

MATT. *(overlapping)* Some men...

DAN. *(overlapping)* No they don't!

MATT. Like Paul McCartney.

DAN. Not Paul! What the hell's the matter with you?

MATT. Look again.

DAN. Oh for cripes' sake!

MATT. I know it's unsettling.

DAN. Unsettling. Yeah. Things are unsettling. Everything here is a little unsettling.

MATT. Yeah... Yeah.

DAN. Yeah... Have you noticed how many statues and angels and cement animals there are around here? Outside, all over.

MATT. They're everywhere.

DAN. And they have bow ties and hats and boots and...

MATT. Arrows and

DAN. Guns.

MATT. Guns?

DAN. No. But you have to be alert. It's...

MATT. Startling.

DAN. Yeah.

> (**JILL** *calls from offstage.*)

JILL. *(offstage)* HELLO!

DAN. *(to offstage* **JILL***)* HEY! *(to* **MATT***)* What do you think about Carol and Jill?

MATT. What about them?

DAN. Have you noticed anything?

MATT. You mean how they look?

DAN. How they look at each other.

MATT. What do you mean?

> (**JILL** *enters with fruit, cutting board, knives, birthday candles. She has a plan.*)

JILL. Hi.

DAN & MATT. Hi.

JILL. I thought you left.

DAN. I came back for the car keys, then Matt and I had a chat and now I'm about to leave, go shoot some...

JILL. Can you wait a second?

MATT. *(to* **JILL***)* What do you have there?

JILL. I want to make a fruit salad since Carol's not eating carbs.

MATT. Fruit salad?

JILL. I thought we could put sixty candles in sixty pieces of fruit.

DAN. Candles in fruit?

JILL. What do you think?

MATT. Carol's not eating carbs?

JILL. Want to help?

MATT. Sure. *(reaches for fruit)* Ow!

JILL. The elbow?

MATT. It's fine.

DAN. So we're making fruit salad instead of a cake?

MATT. There's no cake?

JILL. We can't give her a cake if she's not eating carbs.

DAN. So we're doing fruit.

MATT. Should we go look for her and then do the fruit?

JILL. You could look for her, Matt, and we'll do the fruit.

MATT. I'll help with the fruit. I mean, since she's not eating carbs.

JILL. Did you know Carol gets dizzy when she looks up?

MATT. What?

JILL. Sometimes she gets dizzy. She names things in the room to calm herself down.

DAN. *(to* **JILL***)* Can I use that knife?

JILL. Why?

DAN. This one is dull.

MATT. Carol gets dizzy when she looks up?

JILL. She has dislodged crystals in her inner ear.

MATT. What?

JILL. It goes away on its own. *(to* **DAN***)* Let's share the knife.

DAN. Fine.

JILL. *(to* **DAN***)* Here… Matt?

MATT. What?

JILL. You don't want to help with the fruit?

MATT. Oh. Sure. Fruit.

> *(Lights shift to the lake. We can still see the others in dim light prepping the fruit.)*

Scene Five

(The lake. CAROL enters.)

Matt? HELLO? MATT? Shhh. It's nature.

(looks at lake)

Is that the log?
Log, did Matthew hit you?
Could I hit you?
Where's a rock?

(looks around)

It's all little rocks. Did he throw all the big rocks?
Here's one.

(picks it up, looks at it closely)

Are you going to kiss the rock? Are you going to kiss this rock?

(Looks at it. Kisses it. Puts it to her cheek. Thinks of JILL.)

Oh my… Okay!

(Throws rock. Hits the log.)

What? …I hit it?
Me? The elder?
I hit it! I have to do this again!
Where's a rock…?

(looking around)

Little rocks, little rocks. Should I use two little rocks?
Ping ping.
Here's a good one.

(picks up a rock)

Okay! The markswoman prepares.
She takes a stance.
She sets her sights. On the log. That is the elk.
She…holds the rock to her chest.

She needs to be closer, to the lake.

(moves a bit closer)

A little closer.

(steps closer)

Maybe. Okay. A little...

(steps closer)

Maybe... Oh! Ow!

(She lurches forward, twisting her ankle as she tries to throw. Lights out. Sound of splash, ducks quacking, nature disrupted.)

Scene Six

> *(The lobby. JILL and MATT are creating a platter with birthday candles in pieces of fruit. DAN is standing at the "foul line" across the room, shooting bluberries into the basket that CAROL moved in the first scene. He has moved it to a better spot for "playing ball.")*

DAN. 3-2-1, Swish!

JILL. Dan!

DAN. Two more shots.

JILL. Please stop throwing blueberries into that basket.

MATT. I bet we've done at least sixty candles.

DAN. *(throws)* Yes!

JILL. *(to DAN)* Dan!

MATT. *(to JILL)* Have you been counting?

DAN. *(throws)* Swish!

JILL. *(to MATT)* I've lost track.

MATT. I'll count.

DAN. Now from mid-court! I love this!

JILL. Matt, please tell Dan to stop throwing fruit at the decor.

MATT. Dan…

DAN. The last shot! Jill!

> *(DAN moves to another spot.)*

JILL. Dan!

DAN. Three seconds left!

JILL. *(to MATT)* You counting?

MATT. *(counting)* 21, 22 … *(keeps counting)*

DAN. He moves to the left. He takes the jumper! *(throws)* He scores! Yeeeeesssss! Jill!

JILL. *(paying no attention)* What?

DAN. I won the game! Jill! In the last second!

JILL. Please put the basket back where you found it.

DAN. I didn't move it. *(he did)*

JILL. *(looks up)* You didn't?

DAN. No. *(straightens it – but not in the way it was when* **CAROL** *placed it)*

MATT. 59, 60! ... 61. Better take that one away.

JILL. Give it to me. *(eats fruit)* Should we hide the platter, so Carol won't see?

MATT. Where would we hide it?

DAN. Put it in one of these shelves. It'll blend in.

MATT. She knows what's in the room.

JILL. Why don't we... I'll put it...

> *(***CAROL*** enters. She's wet and disheveled, muddy.)*

CAROL. Hi.

JILL, MATT, DAN. Hi! Hey.

JILL. Welcome back!

MATT. Where you been?

JILL. Are you all wet?

MATT. What happened?

CAROL. I walked into the lake and I, I...

JILL, DAN, MATT. What? Walked into the lake?

MATT. How did you walk into a lake?

JILL. Did you get dizzy?

CAROL. No, I got too close.

MATT. Too close to the lake?

CAROL. I wasn't watching / I was watching, but I wasn't looking and then...

JILL. Are you all right, you look all right. Give me your coat.

CAROL. I pulled my ankle. Who moved that basket?

MATT. Come sit on the couch.

DAN. She can't sit on the couch, she's all wet.

MATT. That doesn't matter!

JILL. Matt, pick her up. You and Dan, pick her up.

DAN. Come on Matt.

JILL. Carol, we'll take you upstairs and we'll…

MATT. I can't pick her up.

CAROL. Matt!

MATT. I can't pick you up.

CAROL. Oh Matt!

DAN. Why not?

JILL. His arm.

CAROL. I asked you to stop throwing rocks!

MATT. Come sit on my lap.

CAROL. Dan, why didn't you stop him from using his arm?

DAN. Why didn't I stop him?!

JILL. Carol, Dan's not going to…

CAROL. I know, sorry Dan. My foot hurts. Matt, will you straighten that basket.

MATT. Basket?

CAROL. Just straighten that basket, please!

MATT. Okay.

JILL. I'll do it! *(picks up basket)*

DAN. Why don't I go pick up something…

CAROL. *(to* **JILL***)* It goes there.

DAN. A compress.

JILL. No wait.

MATT. *(to* **CAROL***)* Hobble over here and sit on my lap.

CAROL. Don't talk to me.

MATT. Come on, honey.

CAROL. I'll stand.

MATT. You shouldn't stand.

CAROL. I'll lean.

JILL. Dan, go get some towels.

DAN. Towels?

JILL. Upstairs.

DAN. *(exiting)* Towels.

CAROL. *(to* **JILL***)* My foot is swollen and the boot's wet. I can't take it off.

MATT. Come sit on my lap.

JILL. You should sit on his lap. I'll help you.

CAROL. Okay okay.

JILL. *(helps her to* MATT*)* We'll dry off the boots and then take it off.

CAROL. If we dry it, won't it tighten?

JILL. I can nudge it.

CAROL. *(to* MATT*)* Why didn't you come look for me?

MATT. I was about to.

CAROL. Sooner!

MATT. I'm sorry. Sit down. *(slaps his lap)*

CAROL. I don't want to. *(she does anyway)*

JILL. DAN! TOWEL!

MATT. Hi honey.

JILL. DAN, PLEASE BRING A TOWEL.

DAN. *(offstage)* ALL THE TOWELS ARE DAMP. HOW ABOUT A BEDSPREAD?

JILL. *(to* CAROL*)* Want a bedspread?

CAROL. No. They're creepy.

JILL. They are?

CAROL & MATT. Yes.

JILL. FORGET THE BEDSPREAD, DAN.

CAROL. *(to* MATT*)* You need this.

> (CAROL *takes off her scarf and puts it around* MATT*'s neck.)*

MATT. What are you doing?

CAROL. Making you a sling.

MATT. I don't think I need…

CAROL. Shut up.

> (CAROL *creates a sling.* DAN *enters.)*

DAN. What's happening?

JILL. Dan, go get my hair dryer.

DAN. Go get?

JILL. My hair dryer.

DAN. Hair dryer – where…

JILL. Maybe my yellow bag.

DAN. Where is…

JILL. Look around / thank you!

DAN. All right! *(exits)*

JILL. Let's take the boot off the foot that doesn't hurt.

CAROL. What is that fruit?

JILL. It's your birthday surprise.

CAROL. Fruit with candles?

MATT. Since you're not eating carbs.

CAROL. Who said, I'm not eating carbs?

JILL. I asked if you wanted corn flakes, you said…

CAROL. Um. I said, "Um."

JILL. I thought…

CAROL. There's no cake?

MATT. I'll go get a cake.

CAROL. You can't drive!

MATT. I can drive.

JILL. Dan can drive.

CAROL. Fruit is fine.

JILL. Dan can go get a cake.

CAROL. We don't need a cake.

MATT. We have charcoal.

JILL. Yes we do.

*(**DAN** enters with hair dryer.)*

DAN. Hair dryer!

JILL. You found it.

DAN. *(holds hair dryer over his head)* I found it!

CAROL. Oh! I looked up! *(dizzy)*

JILL. We have to name things! Quick! …hair!

DAN. What are we doing?

JILL. Naming things in the room, so Carol can ground. Floor!

CAROL. Shoes.

MATT. People!

DAN. Tension.

JILL. No Dan.

MATT. Hair dryer!

JILL. Yes!

CAROL. *(still sitting on* MATT*)* Okay! *(inhales / not dizzy)* Matt, how are your legs? Are they getting numb?

MATT. A little.

CAROL. Do you want me to move to the couch?

MATT. Nooo / unless you want…

JILL. I think she should.

MATT. She could put her foot up.

CAROL. Okay.

> (JILL *helps her to couch*)

CAROL. Matt, do you think your legs are weaker since you fell and haven't been able to exercise…

MATT. I don't know, Carol.

CAROL. Okay.

JILL. Okay! Let's find a plug.

MATT. There's one over here.

DAN. What's the plan?

JILL. I'm plugging this in. We're going to dry Carol off and we'll *(turns on hair dryer)* TAKE OFF HER BOOT, GET HER IN DRY CLOTHES AND THEN WE'LL HAVE DINNER.

CAROL. IT'S TOO HOT.

MATT. TURN IT DOWN.

DAN. SHOULD I MAKE A FIRE?

JILL. LET'S NOT WORRY ABOUT THAT RIGHT NOW.

DAN. I'M NOT WORRIED ABOUT IT.

CAROL. STILL TOO HOT.

JILL. CAROL, SIT STILL!

MATT. TURN IT DOWN!

CAROL. IT'S TOO HOT!! TURN IT OFF!

JILL. WE'RE DOING OUR BEST!!

MATT. TURN IT OFF!!

JILL. OKAY. OKAY! *(Turns it off. She's a little dismayed.)* Remember the summer I turned fifty? …I hiked in the Twin River Range? And it was hot and there was constant wind. It sounded like this.

> *(Turns dryer on. Unintentionally. It's aimed at* **CAROL**'s *head, probably.)*

CAROL. OW!

JILL. *(lost in it a bit)* Sorry. *(turns it off)* It didn't sound like that, it felt like that. But we hiked anyway. I'm not that athletic, but I'm strong and love vistas and I like moving through brush.

CAROL. Jill?

JILL. That was a good group. Everyone was attractive and helpful. Sometimes, it's nice to get away. Isn't it?

CAROL. Maybe it's nice to get away to a place where the wind sounds like a hair dryer, I wouldn't know, and I don't know why we're here.

JILL. What did you expect?

CAROL. I pictured spa things.

JILL. I never said…

CAROL. I know. I guess, I hoped. *(imitates* **JILL**'s *sign for hope / looks up)* Eh. Dizzy.

JILL. We should…

CAROL. Let's not name things!

JILL. Carol.

CAROL. *(looking down)* What?

JILL. This is a nice place.

CAROL. *(still looking down)* It is? *(inhales /dizzy gone)*

JILL. Yes. And we will have a good dinner tonight and we will all give you our gifts. And our love. *(to guys)* Right?

MATT & DAN. *(sheepish)* Right.

DAN. Okay! Hey!

JILL. What?

DAN. I'm going to go.

JILL. No Dan!

DAN. Excuse me?

JILL. *(to DAN)* We don't know about Carol's foot…

DAN. Her foot seems fine, how's your foot, Carol?

CAROL. I'm okay.

MATT. She can't put weight on it.

JILL. She's limping, Dan. *(to CAROL)* Should we take you to the Emergency Room?

CAROL. No no. no. Dan, go ahead, take the car. I'm sorry Matt and I are ruining things with our wounds.

DAN. *(exiting)* I don't mind your wounds.

JILL. Wait!

DAN. No.

JILL. No?

DAN. I need to leave.

JILL. Now?

CAROL. Go ahead, Dan, you can go.

MATT. You need to leave?

DAN. Before I point things out. I'm not usually the one to point things out.

MATT. Sure you are.

DAN. I'm the one who waits to see if my wife will return…

JILL. What?!

MATT. From her trips?

CAROL. Oh God.

DAN. I don't want to point out that I don't know why she goes places she knows little about and always seems slightly ill-prepared. Why does she do that? What's the draw?

JILL. Dan!

MATT. What's the draw?!

JILL. *(to* DAN*)* What's going on?!

DAN. *(to* MATT*)* Is she there for the guides, the Forest Men –
the people who Lead and Rescue?

JILL. Forest Men?

DAN. Maybe it isn't the guides. Maybe it's something closer
to home.

JILL. What are you saying??

MATT. I'm lost.

JILL. Dan, why don't you and I go for a ride. We can talk.
We need to talk... I'll go get my jacket and you have
your jacket, you're wearing your jacket...

DAN. Yes.

JILL. You're ready to go, I'm not ready. How could you not
have said this before? Never mind! I need my jacket!
Wait for me here, or do what you want! Wait in the car,
you decide, you're an adult! Where's my jacket?!!

DAN. In the room.

JILL. Slightly ill-prepared?! What do you mean? How can
you say... Are you just going to stand there?! Where's
my coat? Carol, I'm sorry. Dan! EHHH! Where is my
JACKET?

DAN. It's upstairs!

JILL. Oh... I...oh... *(starts to head upstairs)*

DAN. Jill! I don't mind getting towels for you or finding the
hair dryer or...

JILL. Why are you saying...?

DAN. I don't mind any of that.

MATT. What's happening?

DAN. But I don't like to hike!

JILL. I know.

DAN. I know you know.

JILL. So why...

DAN. Because sometimes I wonder what you do when
you're away on your trips or when I'm out of the room.

JILL. Out of the room?

CAROL. Oh God.

DAN. Do you wonder that, Matt?

MATT. Why would I wonder…?

CAROL. Jill.

JILL. I don't keep secrets!

DAN. You don't?

JILL. There are some things, I have things, I don't say immediately.

DAN. What things?

CAROL. Jill!

MATT. There's a secret?

CAROL. Jill!!

JILL. *(to CAROL)* Wait.

DAN. What's going on between you two?

JILL. Between us?

MATT. Oh no.

CAROL. …We kissed.

MATT. What?

JILL. *(to DAN)* I was going to tell you…

DAN. When?

JILL. It's not something I was planning on not telling you…

MATT. You kissed?

CAROL. Yes.

MATT. They kissed.

DAN. Why?

JILL. It was random.

CAROL. Random?

JILL. Wasn't it?

CAROL. It was…sudden.

JILL. Sudden, yes, out of nowhere.

CAROL. *(to JILL)* But, well, we had been talking about, um…

DAN & MATT. About what?

JILL. Living together.

MATT. Living together?

CAROL. Hypothetically.

MATT & DAN. When we die?!

CAROL. We didn't say that!

MATT. No?

CAROL & JILL. No!

CAROL. And this, what we're saying right now, does not have to interfere, this doesn't need to interfere with our plans for the weekend or with anything.

DAN. What plans?

JILL. Birthday plans.

CAROL. Any plans.

DAN. You kissed?

CAROL & JILL. Yes.

MATT. Carol, aren't you hungry?

CAROL. Hungry? What?

MATT. We have this fruit plate with candles. And I have a gift that isn't the jacket.

CAROL. You remember the jacket.

MATT. I do.

DAN. I knew something was up when I walked in and you two were standing with your foreheads together.

MATT. Foreheads together?

(MATT *puts his hand to his chin.* CAROL *notices.*)

DAN. And I asked you, I did ask you, and you…

JILL. Didn't answer.

DAN. No.

CAROL. Matt. Your hand. Put it down.

MATT. No. Carol.

CAROL. What?

MATT. I'm a man.

CAROL. What?

MATT. *(puts hand down)* My hand. My chin. I'm a man.

CAROL. Please don't say you're a man.

MATT. I am a man.

CAROL. What are you saying?

MATT. My elbow. My hand. My chin. I'm a man.

CAROL. Oh God, again?

JILL. What's happening?

CAROL. Things are collapsing.

JILL. We're horizontal!

DAN. What does that mean?

MATT. My legs! My arm! My socks!! I'm a man.

CAROL. You're a man, yes I heard.

DAN. I'm a man too.

JILL. Oh my God.

MATT. I know I miss things.

DAN. I don't.

MATT. But generally I'm attentive.

DAN. Me too.

MATT. Your gift, for example.

CAROL. My gift?

MATT. I wish I had found the jacket for you that is the exact shade of black that isn't black.

CAROL. Did you look for the jacket?

MATT. I didn't. But I thought about it.

CAROL. Oh Matt.

MATT. Wait, wait, Carol. Listen.

CAROL. Are you going to talk about being a man and buying a gift?

MATT. Yes.

CAROL. I don't want to hear it.

MATT. I want you to know that men sincerely want to give good gifts to their wives. We give it thought, don't we, Dan?

DAN. To be frank, since I discovered moisture free clothes, I haven't worried too much.

JILL. Re-visit that.

DAN. Really?

CAROL. Can we please…!

MATT. Not talk about gifts?

CAROL. Yes.

JILL. So…

MATT. You kissed?

CAROL & JILL. Yes.

DAN. They kissed.

MATT. They kissed each other.

CAROL. We had been talking about…

JILL. An afghan.

CAROL. And we leaned toward each other.

DAN. While discussing an afghan?

JILL. The blanket!

DAN. I understand that.

CAROL. And I said, or maybe you said…

JILL. We didn't say…

CAROL. No.

JILL. And your mouth…

CAROL. My mouth.

JILL. I saw your mouth.

CAROL. Yes.

JILL. Like a peach.

DAN. Peach?

CAROL. Did you think – peach?

MATT. Peach?

JILL. Not at the time.

DAN. You thought peach?!

JILL. Not at the time.

DAN. What does that mean?

MATT. It's a fruit.

DAN. I KNOW IT'S A FRUIT.

CAROL. I know this is asking a lot! But can we please not try to figure it out?

MATT. Then what do you suggest?

CAROL. I don't know.

DAN. I have a suggestion.

JILL. We play basketball.

DAN. If I thought this group would play basketball...

MATT. What's your suggestion?

DAN. ...Why don't we kiss? Matthew?

MATT. What?!

DAN. *(to MATT)* Do you want to kiss?

CAROL. No he doesn't.

MATT. *(to CAROL)* Hold on. *(to DAN)* Dan. You want to kiss me?

JILL. Oh my God.

CAROL. Come on, cut it out.

JILL. Don't mock us.

DAN. Mock you?

MATT. Dan, you want to kiss me?

DAN. Why not?

JILL. Dan!

MATT. I say we kiss!

CAROL. What are you doing?

MATT. Something random?

DAN. Something sudden!

JILL. Something sudden?

DAN. You understand that, don't you, Miss Now I'm Going to Peru Even Though I Just Got Back From Brazil!

JILL. You don't want to travel! You don't like to do things!

DAN. I do different things! What's the point of going somewhere and doing different things?

JILL. We could eat meals together.

DAN. You don't go places where they have places to eat!

JILL. We could eat in the room!

MATT. In the yurt.

DAN. Forget the yurt!

JILL. Yurts aren't bad. They're simple and satisfactory.

CAROL. What is this?! What are we talking about?!!

JILL. When we were in Mongolia...

CAROL. I know about Mongolia!!

MATT. Hey Dan!

DAN. What?

MATT. I say we kiss!

DAN. You think it's time?

JILL. You're going to kiss?

MATT. Are you ready?

DAN. Ready.

JILL. They're going to kiss.

CAROL. Oh my God!

> (**MATT** *and* **DAN** *stand opposite each other –*
> *several feet apart-stock still – they look like they're*
> *about to duel.*)

MATT. Okay.

DAN. Yeah.

MATT. Yeah.

DAN. So how do we do this?

MATT. We need to...

DAN. We need to walk...

MATT. We need to walk toward...

DAN. Each other...

JILL. They're going to walk toward each other.

CAROL. I know.

MATT. We have to...

DAN. Get closer.

MATT. We certainly need to be...

DAN. Closer.

CAROL. Are you going to kiss standing up?

JILL. Don't kiss standing up.

MATT. Still closer.

DAN. Okay.

> *(The men move one at a time, negotiating the space between them. They are doing their best to figure this out.)*

MATT. If I walk… I'll walk… *(takes a step)* here.

DAN. Okay. A step. So I'll step…

JILL. Don't kiss with your bodies… *(places palms together)* close.

CAROL. Matt's arm's in a sling – they can't get too close.

DAN. I'll step over here.

CAROL. *(to JILL)* They're not listening to us.

MATT. *(to DAN)* You walked in a circle.

DAN. Oh right!

MATT. Come closer. Move more aggressively!

DAN. Hey! Don't hog the butch corner!

JILL. Butch!

CAROL. Not now!

MATT. What not now?

CAROL. We talked about roles…

MATT. Roles?!

JILL. She said…because she's brunette…

CAROL. I would be the more butch…

DAN. I would agree with that.

MATT. Wait! Carol! How far did this go?

CAROL. We kissed.

MATT. Where?

CAROL. You mean what room?

DAN. They kissed in this room.

JILL. On the couch.

DAN. No no, I saw you! You were standing right there!

JILL. Not then! We kissed earlier.

CAROL. We kissed this morning.

JILL. We were discussing the – we said that part already...

MATT. The afghan.

DAN. And you kissed.

JILL & CAROL. Right. Yes.

DAN. Are you going to kiss again? Are you going to become kissers?

JILL. We have no plans to become kissers, do we Carol?

CAROL. *(to* JILL*)* No. We have no plans.

DAN. Is that convincing?

MATT. Dan, come on!

DAN. Come on, what?

MATT. Kiss me!

DAN. No.

MATT. Why not?

DAN. Moment's passed.

MATT. Wait! Hold your ground.

DAN. Hold my ground?!

MATT. Close your eyes.

DAN. Don't give me orders. What the hell's the matter with you?

MATT. Oh, I just meant...

DAN. It's all right. I'm a little edgy.

MATT. Sorry.

DAN. I'm sorry too.

MATT. It's okay.

DAN. Okay. I'm closing my eyes.

MATT. Good.

JILL. *(to* CAROL*)* Do you want to watch?

CAROL. I don't know / yes.

DAN. *(to* MATT*)* Do something!

MATT. I'm in charge?

DAN. *(opens eyes)* You're the one who got bossy.

MATT. Okay. Close your eyes.

DAN. You sure?

MATT. Close them. I have an idea.

DAN. *(closes eyes)* Okay.

(**MATT** *takes off the sling –* **CAROL**'s *scarf.*)

CAROL. Matt, no, don't!

DAN. *(eyes closed)* What are you doing?!

MATT. Taking off the sling. *(He untangles it.)*

CAROL. Matt!

DAN. What's going on?!

MATT. *(to* **DAN***)* Don't open your eyes!

JILL. Oh my God!

DAN. *(opens eyes)* What the hell!?

MATT. Close your eyes!

DAN. *(closes eyes)* Okay, okay!

CAROL. Matt, your arm!

MATT. *(to* **CAROL***)* It's okay. *(to* **DAN***)* OKAY. Dan! Ready?

DAN. I think so.

MATT. Okay.

DAN. Okay. Kiss me.

MATT. Okay.

(**MATT** *throws sling around* **DAN**'s *neck / pulls* **DAN** *to him.*)

CAROL & JILL. Oh my God.

(**MATT** *kisses* **DAN** *squarely on the mouth, holding the scarf tight around* **DAN**'s *neck. The kiss lasts a bit longer than expected.*)

JILL. Oo oo.

(They stop kissing.)

DAN. …Okay

MATT. …Yeah.

(**MATT** *steps back, extends his hand to* **DAN**. **DAN**
takes it. They shake hands during:)

DAN. Hey, how are ya?

MATT. I'm all right. How are you?

DAN. I'm okay.

MATT. Good.

(*They stop shaking hands but are still hand-in-
hand.*)

DAN. How were my lips?

MATT. What?

JILL. Dan!

DAN. Were they fat?

CAROL. Hey! Guys!

MATT & DAN. What?

CAROL. Let Go!

MATT & DAN. Right / Okay. (*They drop hands.*) Okay. See
you later.

(*They abruptly turn from each other and walk as
if to exit.*)

JILL. What was that?

MATT. What?

CAROL. You lingered.

DAN. Did we linger?

JILL. You delayed.

MATT. Delayed?

DAN. We shook hands.

CAROL. And delayed.

JILL. With your hands still…

CAROL. Together!

JILL. And I want to know!

CAROL. Want to know what?

JILL. Why they delayed.

MATT. Because…why did we delay, Dan?

CAROL. Because! Because it was an impulse – to kiss and then to shake hands – something out of the ordinary. When something is out of the ordinary there is a delay. Right? That's how it is! There's nothing to it!

DAN. *(to* MATT*)* Was there something to it? Matt?

MATT. *(to* DAN*)* Why did you ask if your lips were fat?

CAROL. *(to* MATT*)* Why are you pursuing this?! Why are you being so dogged and perverse?

DAN. WHAT?!

MATT. *(simultaneous)* You think we're being perverse?!

CAROL. *(overlapping)* I think you're playing around. And you're deliberately making fun of...

MATT. Of what?

CAROL. A situation.

MATT. What situation?

CAROL. A friendship. *(a catch in her voice)* A friendship.

MATT. Are you crying?

CAROL. I'm not crying.

JILL. Carol...?

CAROL. You say you're not mocking, but that's not...!

MATT. Are we mocking, Dan?

DAN. I don't know.

JILL. You don't know?

MATT. Let's kiss again!

CAROL.	JILL.
OHHHH.	No Come on, stop!

MATT. That way we can see if we're mocking or playing or what?

CAROL. Do you want privacy?!

JILL. Don't ask them that!

DAN. Where would we go?

MATT. Over there?

CAROL. The closet?

DAN. I'm not kissing you in a closet.

MATT. I thought that was the Breakfast Room.

CAROL & JILL. The Breakfast Room / is over there.

DAN. Let's stay here. Isn't this the kissing room?

MATT. I guess that's been established.

CAROL. Stop making fun!

DAN. Making fun?

CAROL. Nevermind.

DAN. You going to use the scarf again?

MATT. You liked the scarf?

CAROL. Don't use my scarf!

DAN. Forget the scarf.

CAROL. *(utterly exasperated)* EHHHHHHHHHHHHHH!

JILL. The scarf doesn't matter.

MATT. Carol?

CAROL. What What?

MATT. Did it matter? That is the question.

CAROL. The scarf?

MATT. No the kiss.

CAROL. It was a kiss, *(to* **JILL***)* wasn't it.

JILL. It was.

CAROL. And then, you went for a walk. And I went for a walk.

JILL. You went for a walk?

CAROL. We didn't walk together.

JILL. Where'd you go?

CAROL. To the lake.

MATT. *(to* **CAROL***)* And you found me –

CAROL. Throwing rocks.

MATT. I hit the log, by the way.

CAROL. After I left?

MATT. Yes, after you left, I hit the log.

CAROL. That's sad.

DAN. It's sad?

JILL. What log?

CAROL. In the lake.

MATT. You were saying, Carol…

CAROL. What was the question?

JILL. *(to MATT)* You want to know if it mattered. Right? You both want to know if the kiss mattered… *(to DAN)* You kissed too.

DAN. I did. I kissed a man. An attractive man.

MATT. Thank you.

DAN. No biggie. And…

JILL. And?

DAN. It didn't ring bells.

CAROL. No bells?

DAN. There were no bells.

JILL. Really?

CAROL. Bells, Matt?

MATT. No bells.

DAN. *(to MATT)* Did you think of a peach?

MATT. No!

CAROL. That's what I mean! That's making fun!

DAN. I'm sorry, Carol. *(to JILL)* Jill…?

JILL. *(tender)* What?

DAN. Give us a kiss, honey.

JILL. Now?

DAN. Come on. *(opens arms to her)*

JILL. Oh.

> *(She goes to him.)*

> *(They kiss. MATT and CAROL watch. MATT puts his hand to his chin.)*

CAROL. Matt, hand. *(lightly hits his arm then apologizes)* I'm sorry.

> *(DAN and JILL stop kissing. They look at each other.)*

DAN. How was that?

JILL. You can't compare the kiss from the man you've kissed for thirty years and the woman you kissed this morning in mid-conversation with your hands at your side, can you.

DAN. I don't know.

JILL. It was nice.

DAN. Nice?

MATT. Carol.

CAROL. What?!

MATT. When a man…

CAROL. Oh no.

MATT. When a man gives a gift…

CAROL. We're back to gifts and men and men and gifts…?

MATT. *(overlapping)* When a man gives a gift, he wants you to light up.

CAROL. Okay, Matt. Am I going to light up?

DAN. Oh boy.

JILL. Sh.

MATT. I don't think so.

CAROL. Why not?

MATT. It's not spectacular.

CAROL. No?

MATT. I'm afraid not.

CAROL. So then what do you want?

MATT. Well, when we give our gifts…

CAROL. Do you want me to say? "Thinking about a gift is as good as giving a gift. And I rejoice."

MATT. I think I thought…

CAROL. What…?

MATT. You're very specific.

CAROL. I'm specific.

MATT. You are specific. You know what you like / don't like. You know everything.

DAN. Women know everything.

CAROL. Dan please be quiet.

JILL. It's meant as a compliment, Carol.

CAROL. I know how it's meant. And Matt, I know what it means for you to be sitting there holding your arm to your chest.

MATT. Don't let my arm...it's not bad. It's not the issue.

CAROL. Okay, Matt. You didn't move your arm from your chest, after I told you just now, that you hadn't moved your arm from your chest. The same arm that you cracked when you fell in the hall. The same arm you've been told not to raise over your head. The same arm that you used to throw rocks for what...hours?

MATT. It wasn't hours.

CAROL. It was a long time and now it looks like we're back to square one! Matt! So! Please don't pretend it's okay for you to surrender all good sense because I "know everything!"

MATT. I...well... I needed to...

CAROL. Hit the log!

MATT. Yes.

CAROL. I'm sick of your arm, I'm sorry.

MATT. I know.

CAROL. I hate it, I'm sorry.

MATT. You don't mean it.

CAROL. I mean it.

MATT. I know.

CAROL. And I'm sorry you didn't take time to find something for my sixtieth birthday, even something small.

MATT. I have something small.

CAROL. I don't want something small!

MATT. Carol. Carol.

CAROL. Ai yi yi, what?

MATT. I didn't know your size. And I didn't feel I could ask.

DAN. That's a fact. We talked about it.

CAROL. You talked about my size?

DAN. Jacket size.

MATT. I mean, how can you ask your wife of thirty-two years...

CAROL. I'm a ten. Sometimes an eight.

MATT. Okay. Good to know. Thanks.

CAROL. Oh Matt.

MATT. I...wish... I wish...

CAROL. What?!

MATT. I wish I had THE DAMN JACKET. I WISH I HAD THE JACKET HERE IN THIS ROOM. I WISH YOU COULD OPEN A BOX AND SAY, "OH IT'S THE DAMN JACKET!" "WHAT A SURPRISE!" "WHAT A THOUGHTFUL THING YOU DID, MATT! YOU FIGURED IT OUT. YOU'RE SUCH A GOOD MAN!!" ...OH BOY DO I WISH THAT.

CAROL. ...I know.

MATT. ...I'm sorry.

CAROL. ...Oh my.

DAN. ...What a weekend, huh!

> *(Everyone looks at him. Beat.* **DAN** *takes scarf off his neck.)*

Matt, you want this scarf back?

JILL. It's Carol's.

> *(Everyone looks at* **CAROL.** *)*

DAN. Here you go.

> *(***DAN** *tosses scarf to* **CAROL.** *It falls to the floor. They all look at the scarf. No one moves. then,* **MATT** *picks it up.)*

MATT. Here you go, honey.

> *(He gently wraps the scarf around her shoulders.)*

CAROL. ...You don't want to put this back on your arm...

MATT. No.

CAROL. Will you let me put it back on your...

MATT. No.

CAROL. Okay.

MATT. How are you, Carol?

CAROL. What do you mean?

MATT. How's your foot?

CAROL. My foot?

JILL. Is the boot dry?

CAROL. *(looks at boot)* I don't know. *(looks at* **MATT***)* Matt...

MATT. What?

CAROL. Hi.

MATT. Hi.

CAROL. I hit the log.

JILL. What?

MATT. The log?

JILL. In the lake?

CAROL. Yes.

MATT. Did it drift?

CAROL. I don't know. If it drifted.

MATT. You hit the log?

CAROL. I did.

MATT. Good for you.

CAROL. Twice.

MATT. Twice?

CAROL. I got real close the second time.

MATT. Oh.

CAROL. Does that count?

MATT. ...Yes.

CAROL. Oh... Thank you.

JILL. What does that mean?

DAN. I don't know what it means, but I accept it.

MATT. It means she can feed the tribe.

(A bit of a smile between **MATT** *and* **CAROL**.*)*

JILL. …Okay! I'm hungry!

DAN. Me too!

JILL. Let's eat!

MATT. Good idea!

DAN. I'll go buy the meat!

MATT. I'll go with you.

CAROL. You're not going to drive to Sullivan County!

MATT. *(to* **DAN**) There was a place, remember, nearby, a market…

DAN. *(exiting)* I have a ball in the car, mind if I…one shot, if we see a court?

MATT. *(exiting)* No problem.

> *(Both men turn around and look at the women. Beat.)*

DAN. We're leaving.

JILL. We see that.

> *(A long beat.)*

DAN. Okay.

MATT. Let's go.

> *(They exit.* **CAROL** *and* **JILL** *stare at the door.* **MATT** *and* **DAN** *re-enter.* **MATT** *is happily holding a garden gnome.)*

I found the seventh dwarf!

CAROL. That's not a dwarf, it's a gnome.

MATT. It could be a dwarf.

CAROL. Don't say that, it's wrong.

JILL.	**DAN**.
It's a gnome.	I told him that.

MATT. *(overlapping)* I thought it could be funny, I'll put him back.

CAROL. He can stay.

MATT. You want him to stay?

CAROL. He can have dinner with us.

MATT. Okay! Where should I...?

CAROL. Give him to me.

> (MATT *gives gnome to* CAROL. *She holds it.*)

DAN. Okay, let's go!

JILL. You going to get salmon? *(to* CAROL*)* You want salmon?

CAROL. That's fine.

DAN. You want anything else?

JILL. Get a cake.

DAN. A cake.

CAROL. Don't bother.

MATT. We'll find one.

JILL. Thank you.

DAN. What kind?

MATT. We'll figure it out. Okay. *(turns to leave)*

CAROL. Matt.

MATT. Yes? What?

CAROL. It's not like we're waiting, you know, for you both to die!

JILL. Carol!

MATT. I hope not.

DAN. I thought she was going to talk about the cake.

CAROL. I meant to.

DAN. But you said the thing about dying instead?

CAROL. Yes. I'm sorry. Strawberry.

MATT. Strawberry?

JILL. Strawberry shortcake!

CAROL. That would be nice.

JILL. *(to men)* Get some whipped cream.

MATT. Okay!

CAROL. Thank you.

DAN. Okay! Let's go.

MATT. All right. Back soon.

CAROL & JILL. Okay, thanks, goodbye.

MATT & DAN. Goodbye / See you soon.

CAROL & JILL. Goodbye.

>*(DAN and MATT exit. CAROL and JILL look at each other.)*

JILL. Hi.

CAROL. Yeah.

JILL. Well…

CAROL. Did you stop talking?

JILL. I didn't stop talking.

CAROL. It seemed like you weren't talking.

JILL. I talked.

CAROL. …Okay.

JILL. Just a minute.

CAROL. Where are you going?

JILL. Wait here. I'll be right back.

>*(JILL exits. CAROL's holding the gnome. She sets it down. She takes off her scarf and decorates the gnome – parties it up. JILL returns with her gift. She looks at gnome.)*

That looks nice.

CAROL. Thank you… What's that? *(referring to gift)*

JILL. Your fucking birthday. With love.

CAROL. Thanks.

>*(She takes gift, crosses to couch. Sits, opens it. She pulls out a portion of the afghan and puts it back.)*

Thank you.

>*(JILL perches near CAROL.)*

JILL. You cold?

CAROL. Not really.

JILL. You want some fruit?

CAROL. It has candles in it.

JILL. You think it'll taste waxy?

CAROL. It might.

JILL. Want something else? Tea?

CAROL. I don't think so, no thanks...

> *(They're close. Their position suggests or mirrors their positon when they kissed. They linger. Then they look away. Beat.)*

JILL. Funny.

CAROL. What?

JILL. I don't know.

CAROL. How it grabbed us like that.

JILL. Yeah... You like strawberry cake?

CAROL. I think so.

JILL. *(turns to CAROL)* I didn't know that.

CAROL. *(out of words; turns to JILL)*

JILL. *(nothing to say either; half-hearted laugh)*

CAROL. *(another half-hearted laugh)*

CAROL & JILL. *(laugh fades away)*

> *(Slowly, they look away from each other, as the lights fade to black.)*

End of Play